At the

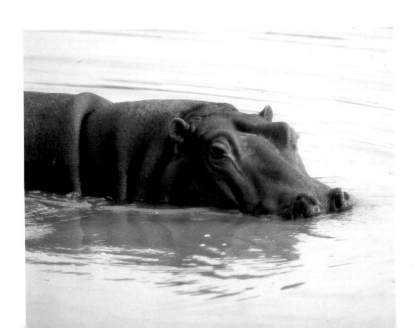

Come and see

the monkey.

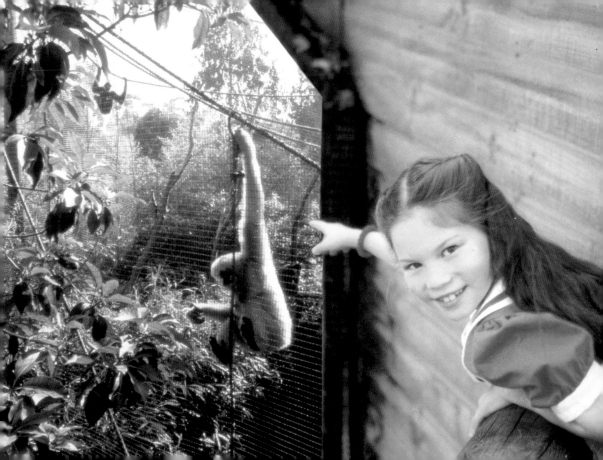

Come and see
the elephant.

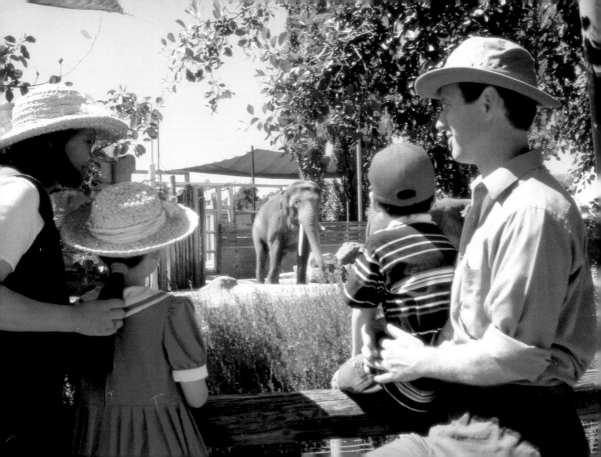

Come and see

the kangaroos.

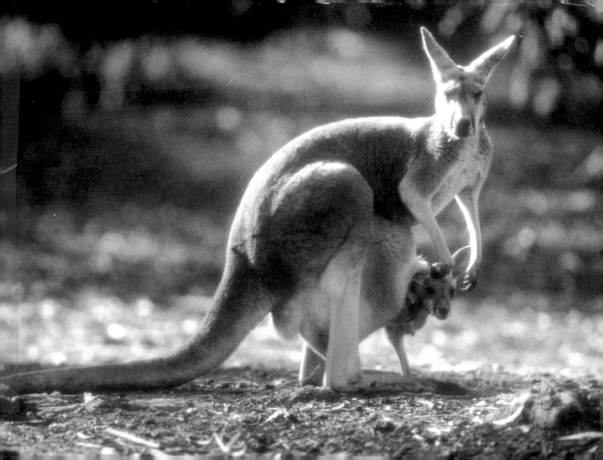

Come and see
the tiger.

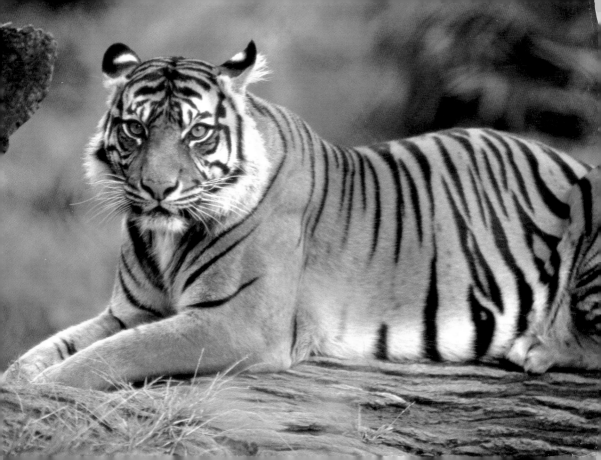

Come and see

the bear.

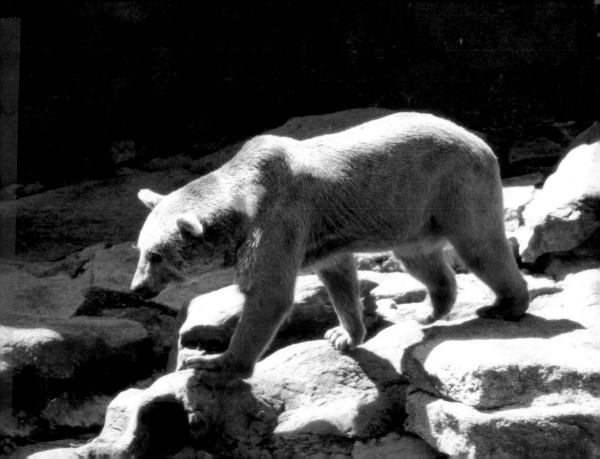

Come and see
the giraffe.

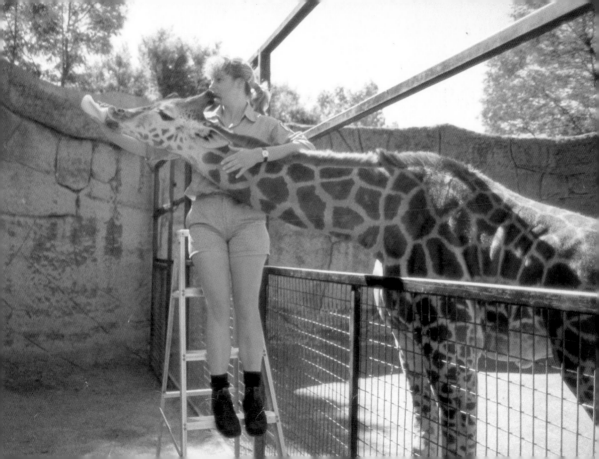

Come and see
the zebra.

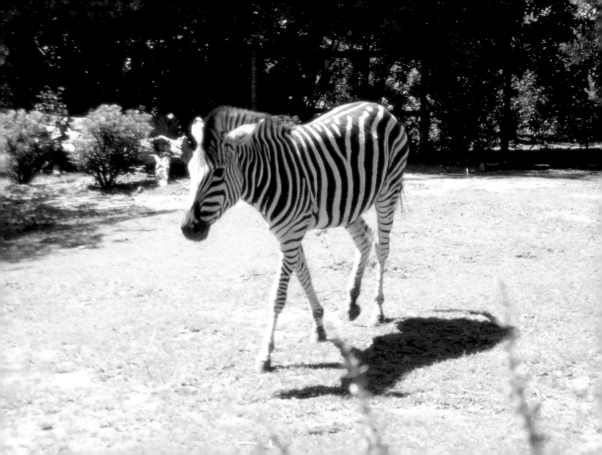

Come and see

the hippopotamus.

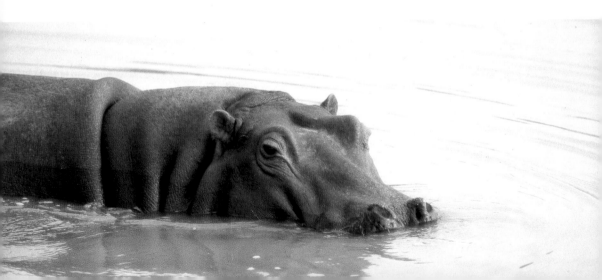